FATAL PODCAST

By

Prism Thomas

G. STEMPIEN PUBLISHING COMPANY

Newport, Wales

ISBN 978-0-930472-91-7

Copyright © Prism Thomas 2025

3

CONTENTS

DEAD AT THE LAPTOP

A Basic den in a modern, average Los Angeles bungalow type house in the late afternoon. DEBBIE BORGES, EARLY 30's, ATTRACTIVE, FEMALE, PARTICULARLY INNOCENT FACE, LIGHT COMPLECTED, STRAIGHT BLONDE HAIR is dead and drooped forward onto a computer desk, with one hand still splayed across the keyboard which is strewn with pills. The face on the computer screen is MAXXUS. A MALE, LATE 30'S, EXCEPTIONALLY ATTRACTIVE BUT A CLEARLY PSYCHOTIC INDIVIDUAL as seen in his eyes. He is speaking but the sound is muted.

LT. DETECTIVE SID MYERS - MID 50'S, AVERAGE BUILD, THICK GREY/BROWN HAIR, SEVERELY DETERMINED TYPE, and his assistant, DETECTIVE SGT. RISA SANCHEZ - EARLY 30'S, short reddish/brown hair, 3rd generation Hispanic, are both on the scene.

RISA
Overdose?

Sid picks up an empty pill bottle from the desk by inserting a pencil tip into the bottle.

SID
Would be my guess.

RISA
Suicide then?

SID
Of a type.

RISA
What does that mean, Sid, uh Lieutenant Myers?

Sid sets the pill bottle back down, and uses the eraser head of the same pencil to draw over from the edge of the desk a piece of paper that had been printed on and written on and was removed from the nearby printer.

SID
Obvious suicide note. "I can't live without you, Maxxus. How could I have betrayed you? Maybe my death will make up for it."

RISA
What's written on the bottom?

SID
A note by the victim reminding her to take her daughter to soccer practice later today. Looks like there won't be any later.

RISA
What was the name of the person she was addressing in that note...the one she betrayed?

SID
Maxxus.

RISA
Maxxus. I've heard that name. Some kind of guru, politician, podcaster...whatever.

SID
A lunatic by any other name.

The face of Maxxus appears, frozen as last seen on the laptop screen as Sid pauses the running program.

RISA
I've seen his picture somewhere.

SID
We've had many complaints. He's a psychopath and sadist who preys on abused women. Claims to be able to show them the direct route to God.

RISA
Sounds like a con man, bunco artist to me.

SID
He's got quite a following on his podcast. Millions I hear. There's even talk about a political future for him - maybe president.

RISA
What! Him?

SID
Sure. A huge, hypnotized and brainwashed voting block. Perfect.

RISA
Aren't most voters hypnotized in one way or another?

SID
Sure, but not as deeply as this guy does it.

RISA
Do we have anything on our suicide victim yet? How was she connected to this Maxxus?

SID
She did some type of PR and communications work. Her last message from him on the laptop might help explain.

Sid turns on the program and the monitor's sound. The view shifts back and forth among the detectives and the face on the computer monitor.

MAXXUS
(from monitor - deep voice)
I can't trust you any more, Debbie. You were supposed to be spreading my name...the message. Not my secrets! I'm glad I stopped you in time. Debbie, you are cast out! Forever!

RISA
Cast out? How medieval.

SID
It's a cult. Religion of a type mixed with politics. The gullible fall for it.

RISA
But all you have to do is...this. She turns off the monitor.

SID
Not that simple. If you are a ready made victim you are already hooked in. And then there are hypnotic suggestions he slips in along with other subliminals.

RISA
Why? I mean, what does he get out of all of this?

SID
Contributions from the hypnotized followers. A sense of power. And all of the free sex he can ever want. Molestation was what the complaints were about.

Sid notices something the dead woman is clutching in her left hand. He gently pries open her still flaccid hand and removes a small, circular metallic medallion from it. CLOSE UP of medallion reveals a militaristic type symbol on it.

RISA
What's that?

SID
Some type of military insignia. The symbolism isn't familiar to me.

Sid motions one of the evidence collection crew over to him and drops it into the plastic bag the officer instantly holds out.

SID
Have them identify that.

The man nods and starts away. As he does he is passed by an excited seven-year-old girl rushing into the room, holding up a drawing she had made on a piece of paper.

GIRL
Mommy! Mommy, look what I drew for you in class today!

Risa catches the little girl into her arms before she can reach her dead mother's body. She then carries the now screaming girl out of the room and places her in the arms of a uniformed police officer.

SID (to officer)
Damn it, why did you let that girl in here!

OFFICER
Sorry, sir, but she ran past me before I even knew she'd come in the door.

SID
Get her away from here.

The police officer carries away the girl. Sid goes back to the monitor, freezes it and mutes it. Sid leans directly into the monitor screen, shoving the suicide paper at the image on it.

SID
(rage)
One way or another, I'm going to get you, you damn son-of-a-bitch!

Risa interrupts him. Sid leans back from the screen.

SID

I had a younger sister - Elaine. She got trapped in a cult by a lunatic like this. I was still in the police academy and didn't really know what was happening at the time.

RISA

How is your sister now? Did she get out?

SID

In a way. She's dead.

RISA

(stammering)

I...I'm so sorry, Sid. I didn't know.

SID

The head of the cult was a narcissistic sex fiend just like this Maxxus guy. An irate husband killed him. Good thing he got to him before I could.

RISA

Sounds like justice.

SID

Our records say that the victim has a husband named Robert in the military stationed in Germany. But the military has no record of him. Sid picks up, folds the suicide note and sticks it in his pocket.

RISA
Detective Myers: that's evidence. Shouldn't it be bagged and sent to the department.

Sid becomes a solid block and stares down at Risa with an expression which says, "I am going to perform this investigation MY way. It will be legal. But I am going to make this man pay."

In a dead silence, Risa - the lieutenant's subordinate - stares back upward at him. At first, her expression is uncertain. Then her expression changes and should be interpreted as: "I understand and not only will not interfere but will help you. He must be stopped."

RISA
You know, the victim reminds me of my mother. She used to take me to soccer practice. I could've been that little girl who just ran in here.

SID
(facing monitor)
I am going to jam that suicide note right in that madman's face!

Sid bends over, picks up a pen and writes a message on a piece of paper that's next to the computer. He then summons a police officer over to him, then hands him the paper.

SID ((to officer)
His name is Maxxus First. I want him in for questioning on a murder investigation.

The officer departs.

RISA
I'd love to personally get that bastard who made this little girl an orphan.

SID
You must've read my mind.

RISA
What do you mean?

SID
We're going to need an undercover operator to catch him. It has to be a woman.

RISA
I have the qualifications for that.

SID
Even more than you think. You have a background in public relations and tech services, don't you?

RISA
Are you kidding? The department trained me for that position. I transferred later to patrol work.

SID
I think you're about to put that earlier department training to very good use.

Sid leads Risa toward the door.

THE INTERROGATION

Inside the typical looking interrogation room at a Los Angeles police station.

Four people sit in attendance at the questioning of Maxxus: Sid, Maxxus, his ATTORNEY, NONDESCRIPT, LATE 30's, and the Department's Head clinical psychologist DR. TED FRIEDMAN, MEDIUM BUILD, LATE 50's, MUSTACHE, CIVILIAN ATTIRE. All are seated at a small table in an enclosed room which is under video observation from above.

MAXXUS
Why have I been dragged in here? Another delusional female again?

SID
A dead female.

MAXXUS
Dead? Who?

SID

Ever heard of a woman by the name of Debbie Borges?

MAXXUS

Sure. She works for me.

SID

Not any more. She resigned the hard way earlier today.

MAXXUS

So why am I here?

SID

You were the last person to communicate with her. It's police procedure to question the people who were the last to have contact with a victim of a suspicious death.

MAXXUS

The last time I talked to her was over the laptop.

SID

It qualifies as a virtual contact because at the time it was a live transmission between the 2 of you and it was saved to the screen by the victim's final act of life. We call that a dying clue.

MAXXUS

This isn't a cheap detective novel, you know.

SID
Facts are facts. The victim's last act was to freeze the
monitor screen on the person to whom she was speaking.
You!

MAXXUS
Even you are smart enough to know that I couldn't have
killed her over the monitor screen.

ATTORNEY (to Sid)
(interposing)
I understood that it was ruled a suicide.

SID
It's ruled a suspicious death. And suicides can be induced
which makes it murder.

ATTORNEY
Even so, you need hard evidence to establish that
charge.

Ignoring him, Sid sifts through some papers before him.

SID (to Maxxus)
The victim worked for you?

MAXXUS
(biting his word)
Yes. I already said so.

SID

What did she do?

MAXXUS
She was in charge of PR, communications and producing my daily Podcast.

SID
Sounds like a pretty responsible position for you to seem unaffected by her sudden...resignation.

MAXXUS
(angry)
She's dead, man! Dead. She didn't resign.

SID
Did she have access to sensitive information concerning your organization?

MAXXUS
Yes, I'd say so.

SID
Was it by the unauthorized misuse of this information that you claimed she betrayed you?

MAXXUS
(very angry)
What!

SID
This!

Sid shoves the suicide paper left by Mrs. Borges in the face of Maxxus.

ATTORNEY (to Sid)
I'm advising my client not to respond to that last question.

SID (to both men)
I have to caution you that we have heard the last communication between the victim and her employer.

ATTORNEY
Noted.

SID (to Maxxus)
Have you any knowledge of what was the content of the secret that the victim had planned to divulge?

ATTORNEY
I advise my client not to respond.

SID (to Maxxus)
How long did the victim work for you in her final capacity?

MAXXUS
About 7 years.

SID
Were you intimate with her at any time during those years or before?

ATTORNEY

I advise my client not…

SID (to Maxxus - cutting off attorney).
Did her husband know of his wife's close association with your organization?

MAXXUS
(grinding his jaw)
I don't know. We never discussed him.

SID
(incredulous)
In 7 years time you never discussed her husband with the victim!

ATTORNEY
(forcefully interposing)
What is the purpose of this insulting line of questioning?

SID
To establish the type of relationship between the victim and your client. Was it completely platonic or something more?

ATTORNEY
I don't see the relevance. I advise my client not to answer any questions of this type.

SID (to Maxxus)
You do know that the victim had a 7 year old daughter?

MAXXUS
Yes, she often spoke of her.

SID
Is she your daughter?

Maxxus shoots upward in his seat.

ATTORNEY
(growling)
That's enough, Lieutenant Myers! You are going too far.

Sid shuffles through more papers and Maxxus resumes his seat.

Dr. Friedman now enters the conversation.

DR. FRIEDMAN (to Maxxus)
I'm curious about something, Mr. First. That is your correct, legal surname is it not?

MAXXUS
Yes. Maxxus First.

DR. FRIEDMAN
About the usage of the word "cast out" in your communication with the victim: kind of archaic, isn't it?

Maxxus only shrugs.

DR. FRIEDMAN
Or does it have some special significance? Like a biblical term of separation.

MAXXUS

If you say.

DR. FRIEDMAN
And to be "cast out forever" as your message states implies a kind of finality. Sort of like a judgment.

MAXXUS
Make of it anything you like. But we are a semi-religious organization. Biblical is proper for us.

DR. FRIEDMAN
You must acknowledge though that, as a cult leader…

MAXXUS
(interrupting)
We are not a cult.

DR. FRIEDMAN
As you wish. But the words "Cast out Forever" delivered by you have a connotation of judgment and separation. Don't you think that the victim heard it that way?

MAXXUS
I have no idea what was going through her mind.

DR. FRIEDMAN
(sarcastically)
Really? Isn't it your modus operandi to prepare the minds of your followers to accept your words as godly commands?

ATTORNEY
(angrily)

I object to this whole process at this point. It is bordering on intimidation!

Sid glares at both men and pounds the desk

.

SID
Believe me, you'd know if and when you are being intimidated.

ATTORNEY
Do you need us for anything else?

SID
No, your client is not being charged at this time. But I advise him not to leave the state.

Maxxus and his attorney fight from their seats and bolt out the door.

DR. FRIEDMAN
I'd sure like to know how he's doing it?

SID
Doing what, doctor?

DR. FRIEDMAN
So thoroughly brainwashing his followers. He's using some technique beyond the basic subliminal suggestion.

SID
Well, that's what we hope Risa is going to find out for us.

DR. FRIEDMAN
So that's why she didn't attend this questioning. She'll be undercover.

SID
If the captain agrees with my proposal. I've made an appointment with him to discuss the idea.

DR. FRIEDMAN
You do have this all planned out, don't you?

SID
All I know is that I'm going to get evidence - hard evidence - that connects Maxxus with this murder. And the most likely place it will be found is in his own personal data.

Outside the building, Maxxus and his attorney walk into the midst of a group of about 100 supporters. They carry signage of support, some of which read: STOP PERSECUTING MAXXUS; SALVATION NOW; MAXXUS FOR PRESIDENT; etc.

Maxxus stops to address them, as police gather.

MAXXUS
It's great to see all of you here in support. Those of us who spread the word of brotherhood and salvation must expect harassment. But it will not stop us.
.
Shouts of encouragement.

MAXXUS

They can't ignore your combined voices and your plea for justice. They may drag me down the streets like they did to Jesus but God is always watching and is preparing a day for our deliverance.

A great cheer erupts. Then there comes the crack of gunfire. One shot rings out. The crowd scatters in panic. Maxxus' attorney shrinks to the pavement and police in the vicinity rush to the scene but cannot find the shooter. Officers also spring from inside the building, including Sid. He rushes to Maxxus and his attorney.

SID (to Maxxus)
Looks like you've made an enemy.

MAXXUS
Not everyone agrees with the truth of my words.

SID
Or having their wives, daughters and sisters brainwashed.

ATTORNEY (to Sid)
My client is the victim here.

MAXXUS (to Sid)
I ought to sue the department - being fired upon right outside your front doors.

SID

Maybe that's why he missed. We made the shooter nervous.

ATTORNEY (to Maxxus)
Come on, let's get down to my office.

SID (to both)
Do you need a ride to your destination? The shooter might still be in the area.

ATTORNEY
No, thanks detective. My office is just down the street.

SID
I'll send some officers with you anyway just to be safe.

Sid motions to a group of nearby uniformed officers and tells them: See that they have an escort to their destination down the street, will you?

Maxxus and his attorney are escorted by a squad of police from the area.

TESTING RISA

Detective Risa Sanchex enters Dr. Friedman's office at the police station. It's a compact sized office common to a medical specialist's. Risa takes a seat before the desk of Doctor Friedman. Only the 2 of them are present.

DR. FRIEDMAN
I discussed your proposed undercover assignment with the Captain and he gave his permission but only upon my approval.

RISA
And I am here to argue my case?

DR. FRIEDMAN
More or less. But what I really want to do is make sure that because of your relative inexperience with performing undercover assignments that you are clearly aware of the dangers you will be facing.

RISA
I have a pretty good idea of the target's M.O.

DR. FRIEDMAN
The danger I'm talking about is danger to the mind. You need to know the depths of the subject's psychosis and exceptional mental force.

RISA
Any information you could add would be welcome.

The doctor opens the large desk drawer at the front of his desk and takes out 4 drawings made by a department sketch artist. He carefully - methodically - lays them out side by side on his desktop, facing Risa.

DR. FRIEDMAN
This might impress you.

RISA
Four very similar looking males.

DR. FRIEDMAN
Look more closely.

Risa does as suggested, but then sits back and shrugs.

DR. FRIEDMAN
These drawings are all of the same person each made within 5 months of one another. Each one is a drawing of Maxxus.

RISA
He's a master of disguise?

DR. FRIEDMAN
In a manner of speaking.

The doctor returns the drawings to his desk drawer.

RISA
I don't quite understand. The use of disguises by perps is pretty common.

DR. FRIEDMAN

Not so in this case. Maxxus is far more than a simple disguise artist.

Risa
Oh?

DR. FRIEDMAN continues
These descriptions of Maxxus were given by 4 different females only months apart, all of whom claimed he molested them. One reason we couldn't charge Maxxus was because the descriptions varied by such a degree.

RISA
Were they drawn by different sketch artists?

DR. FRIEDMAN
All were drawn by Reggie of this precinct

.

RISA
They must be accurate then. Reggie is a true artist. Then, again, I'd guess that Maxxus was wearing a disguise in each case.

DR. FRIEDMAN
No, the drawings represent his actual physical appearance as seen by the 4 complainants.

RISA
Then what are you saying?

DR. FRIEDMAN

That the minds of the 4 females in question were either so deranged by contact with Maxxus that they couldn't accurately describe his face. Each of them literally saw a slightly different face.

RISA
Impressive.

DR. FRIEDMAN
Here's more. Look at these mugshots next.

Ted withdraws 4 photographs from a side drawer and lays them out before Risa as he'd done the drawings. They are all different likenesses of Maxxus.

DR. FRIEDMAN
Cameras don't lie or make mistakes.

RISA
So what does all of this mean?

DR. FRIEDMAN
Either, that our best sketch artist suddenly lost his abilities while drawing this individual and the mugshot cameras all malfunctioned in his presence, or…

RISA
Neither of which seems likely

DR. FRIEDMAN
Or that Maxxus has the ability to cause people and electronic devices to view him as either he wishes them to or how they would like to imagine he looks.

RISA
Is...is that even possible?

DR. FRIEDMAN
Theoretically. It's like a process known as fascination where a mind that is powerful enough can overwhelm the consciousnesses of others to make them view the subject as they'd like them to. That includes body type as well as facial features.

RISA
And you believe that Maxxus has this ability?

DR. FRIEDMAN
Almost certainly. We are dealing with a narcissistic psychopath who possesses a hyper IQ. He may be able to perform acts that seem magical or miraculous to the untrained observer.

RISA
This all might be true, but I have a particularly powerful motivation to stop this madman which might counteract his so-called abilities.

DR. FRIEDMAN

Yes, Lt. Myers informed me of your close relationship with your late mother and the similarity with the death of Ms. Barges and her daughter.

RISA
I pictured myself hurrying home to show my mother a picture I'd drawn for her in class to find her murdered. And my mother used to love taking me to soccer practice.

DR. FRIEDMAN
But this personal association could also be a detriment. You will need to be as clear thinking as possible to handle this assignment.

RISA
I know.

DR. FRIEDMAN
Do you? This is your first solo undercover mission. There will be no escape routes. If he learns your true identity or simply gets angry at you he will show no mercy. He has no conscience.

RISA
The department trained me well in self defense. I have a black belt in karate.

DR. FRIEDMAN
And Maxxus will have the super physical rage and the force of insanity behind him.

RISA
It would be quite a physical test.

DR. FRIEDMAN
No, it's a test you have to try to avoid at all costs. You must know that the true strength of karate defense is knowing that you may never need to use it. I have a black belt in jiu jitsu myself, but never expect to use it.

Risa nods.

DR. FRIEDMAN
You will also have to be on guard for the psychological damage that Maxxus can cause.

RISA
Karate also trains us in mental discipline.

DR. FRIEDMAN
Bravado can lead to chaotic thinking. I have been following the career of Maxxus for years and he falls into one of the most unique of categories. I need you to truly understand the depth of his awesome power.

RISA (surprise)
Awesome, doctor? You sound almost like a disciple of his.

DR. FRIEDMAN
Know thy enemy. I have studied cases where he has twisted reality and deranged individual's thinking so that they were no longer even aware of their own identity. He's something like a savant, but his mental control is of an even more exceptional and evil nature.

RISA
Now it sounds like you're trying to scare me.

DR. FRIEDMAN
I am. The problem is that the very qualities that make you uniquely prepared for this assignment make you as uniquely vulnerable as well.

RISA
Oh?

DR. FRIEDMAN
Our target - Maxxus - is used to overcoming the wills of women of average ability. But to be faced by a powerful female both mentally and physically is a challenge his type cannot possibly resist.

RISA
I see.

DR. FRIEDMAN
His goal will be to break you. He hates all women, especially the independent ones. And your single mindedness of purpose will for once in his life keep him off balance.

RISA
That's a good thing.

DR. FRIEDMAN

It can be. But it can also be extremely dangerous. A person of his type when off balance may also strike out more suddenly and forcefully.

RISA
I understand. But I'm not sure now what I'm supposed to say.

DR. FRIEDMAN
That you are aware that you have never met anyone of his type and he is dangerous no matter what type of training you've had.

RISA
I understand.

DR. FRIEDMAN
There's still one last thing. There is a wavelength of madness emitted by people like Maxxus and you can become affected by it.

RISA
You mean be driven mad by mere proximity to him?

DR. FRIEDMAN
Yes, for any length of time. It's a medical fact. You won't cure him. But he can mentally damage you.

RISA
(nods)
Again - understood.
DR. FRIEDMAN
(stares into her eyes)

Yes, I believe you do.

RISA
So, what next?

DR. FRIEDMAN
Show up at Maxxus' office early tomorrow morning to apply for Ms. Borges's former PR position. The department has made arrangements with all local news outlets to allow you access to all of their facilities once needed.

RISA
Then my official role as I understand it will be to perform PR for Maxxus and be tech advisor on his podcasts.

DR. FRIEDMAN
Yes, and to be as brass as possible to the target. It'll both intrigue and confuse him, but be careful not to cross the line and enrage him.

RISA
That is a fine line.

DR. FRIEDMAN
Keep in mind that we're looking for evidence linking him to the Barges killing and that information will probably be associated with his unique brainwashing method.

RISA

Right.

DR. FRIEDMAN
And remember this: if you do uncover his secret you'll receive the same violent reaction as Ms. Barges. His reaction will be sudden and brutal.

RISA
Understood.

DR. FRIEDMAN
Okay, then I'll contact the captain and he can give you details on timing and who you'll be coordinating with.

Risa stands up, but before departing she motions toward an item on the top shelf of one of the short bookcases in the room. It's a spiral shaped device the size of a dartboard that is set upon a small stand.

DR. FRIEDMAN
Something else, Sergeant?

RISA
Yes, that object on your bookcase. It looks like something I'd see in a hobby shop or some place like that. It looks familiar.

DR. FRIEDMAN
Oh, that? Does it make you dizzy or off balance to look at?

RISA

No. It just seems a curious thing to be in a clinical psychologist's office.

DR. FRIEDMAN
It's similar to what used to be known as a hypnotic spiral or wheel. I use it to determine if anyone who comes into my office might be suffering from organic brain syndrome.

RISA
What do you do - spin it or something?

DR. FRIEDMAN
No, it's not moveable. If a person who has organic brain syndrome peers at the wheel it would make him very dizzy just by looking at it.

RISA
I see. It doesn't have that effect on me. My mother saw a toy like that at a carnival a long time ago and bought me one. Not quite the same as yours but close enough.

She digs into her purse and withdraws a miniature type item very similar to the Doctor's. She shows it to him briefly.

RISA
I keep it in my purse as a remembrance of that beautiful day we spent together.

DR. FRIEDMAN

Ah, that helps me see even clearer why you're so involved in the Barges case.

The telephone on Ted's desk rings. He picks up the receiver, engages in a brief one-sided communication, then hangs up.

DR. FRIEDMAN
They're ready for you at processing.

RISA
Thanks for approving me for the assignment.

Risa takes a final glance at the spiral wheel on the bookcase, then departs.

PODCAST STUDIO

An office which looks more like a mini movie theatre with rows of seats facing a raised and enclosed podcast studio. On the outside wall of the studio is a wall viewing screen on which the podcast is projected when in process.

Risa sits alone in one of the theater type seats and watches Maxxus perform his current podcast on the viewing screen. She is dressed in seductive business attire. The viewing screen becomes dark just after Risa's entrance.

A moment later Maxxus bursts out from the podcast chamber and descends the short ramp that leads to the theatre area below. Risa stands and walks toward him. Her initial impression of Maxxus is of a powerful severe looking young man who is somewhat handsome. It is a product of "fascination" and as such is the impression he is projecting to her.

MAXXUS
How'd you get in here?

RISA

Your receptionist let me in. I told her I was here to interview for her position. She seemed quite anxious to let me in.

MAXXUS
Quite a smart ass. You need a lesson in speaking to your superiors.

RISA
And you need a good publicist to convince the gullible of your superiority.

MAXXUS
(sarcastically)
And I'm sure you know just the person.

RISA
Sure. But she'd never work for a person like you. Now me on the other hand...

MAXXUS
You'd be a great publicist, I assume.

RISA
See, you already recognize that fact.

MAXXUS
What - are you doing a vaudeville routine now?

RISA
No, but you seem to be doing one here.

MAXXUS

What's that supposed to mean?

RISA
You're hardly getting any newsworthy exposure at all. Especially with all that's happened to you lately.

MAXXUS
And you can fix that?

RISA
Hell yeah. That's my business.

MAXXUS
Okay. Give me a for instance.

RISA
Easy. Somebody took a shot at you yesterday. I didn't hear anything about it in the paper, on tv, or anywhere.

MAXXUS
Then how did you know about it? Unless you're the one who took that shot at me.

RISA
Believe me - I would if there'd be good publicity from it for either of us.

MAXXUS
Again, so how did you know about the shooting?

RISA

I have a very close friend who works on the LA TIMES and covers the LAPD beat. He tells me items like that. Contacts are vital in my business. And I have them.

MAXXUS
So what would you have done with that item?

RISA
I would've made it a big story in the papers and local tv. I've got the connections.

MAXXUS
Okay, you might be worth looking at for the job. Official interviews for my new PR person are in the morning.

RISA
(ignoring him)
I also heard you were hauled in for questioning about the so-called suicide of your former publicist and assistant.

MAXXUS
People are hauled in everyday for questioning.

RISA
Not of your stature.

MAXXUS
(grins egotistically)
So, I have stature.

RISA

But it could be a lot larger if you don't rely only on your podcast for notoriety.

MAXXUS
At last count I have about 6 million followers.

RISA
You wouldn't mind tripling that - or more - would you?

MAXXUS
Sounds good. How?

RISA
Just as an example: right after you left the police department after the questioning I would've arranged for a press conference with you and your attorney. That's the kind of thing that gets you wide attention.

MAXXUS
I have to admit, a press conference would've been good.

RISA
Yeah, and what if during that press conference someone took a shot at you as actually happened. Think of the publicity! You would've been front page.

MAXXUS
Okay, you are making sense.

Maxxus stands closer to Risa, puts a hand on her shoulder which gives her a mild shock. She winces from it and is surprised by it.

RISA
You've got quite a touch.
MAXXUS
I affect people of intelligence that way.

RISA
Animal magnetism, huh?

MAXXUS
Now if you were to come home with me tonight, you'd be sure to be the first person interviewed in the morning.

RISA
Maybe, but would I be sure to get the job?

MAXXUS
You'd head the list.

RISA
Sorry, I want a sure thing.

Risa starts toward the door. Maxxus follows her closely, peering down on her with eyes which feel to her as if they are pressing down upon her.

MAXXUS
I'd say that you need me a lot more than I need you.

RISA
You need a dialog coach.

Risa uncomfortably digs into her handbag and withdraws a business card. She hands it to Maxxus who awkwardly bumps a finger into the edge of it before taking it. It was purposefully meant to put her mentally off balance.

MAXXUS
You need me to make the news for you. That'll catapult your career.

RISA
Yes, I do admit that. The next move is up to you.

MAXXUS
Every move is up to me.

RISA
Most men feel that way.

MAXXUS
We'll do this. I'll check out your credentials. Then, if you do check out, we'll meet tomorrow at Crossroads Kitchen. That's one of the top eating places on Melrose. Give me your mobile number and I'll let you know.

RISA
Fair enough. Crossroads Kitchen tomorrow. Phone number is on my card. And you're paying.

As Risa exits, Maxxus peers down at her business card and flicks a devious glare toward her.

SHOOTER IN THE BUILDING

A large force of Los Angeles police have cordoned off an old fashioned 3 story former toy warehouse. Lt. Myers drives up in his unmarked car accompanied by Risa's temporary replacement SGT. Carlos Montoya. Early 40's, average height, Hispanic heritage. The 2 men walk over to the sergeant in charge of the area, SAM ROONEY, a nondescript man in mid 40's.

SID (to Rooney)
Hi, sergeant, what've we got here?

ROONEY
It seems that we tracked down the guy who took a shot at that Maxxus person yesterday. That's why I asked for you.

SID
Odd to track him a day later. And so far from the shooting.

ROONEY
Yeah, strange. It's sort of like he wants us to find him.

SID
Or maybe he's leading us into a trap.

ROONEY

Yeah, and that abandoned toy warehouse he's in is quite a trap.

SID
Has he taken a shot at anybody since you pursued him?

ROONEY
No, that's the weird thing. He was spotted by some citizens running down El Camino drive with a rifle and we followed him here. But he hasn't fired a shot.

SID
Sounds like he's either high or crazy. Not a lot of people run down El Camino drive carrying rifles.

ROONEY
Dangerous for sure.

A glare or reflected light appears in an upstairs window. Sid points toward it.

SID
Must be our shooter.

ROONEY
Or an accomplice of his, setting up a crossfire.

SID
Well, standing around here won't accomplish anything. I think I'll take a chance that this isn't a trap.

ROONEY
That's a pretty big risk.

SID
Have your men keep a tight cordon around the building
and have tear gas ready if things break.

ROONEY
They'll be ready.

CARLOS (to Sid)
Want me to go in with you?

SID
No, that might scare the guy in case he wants to talk. But
I do want you to come with me to the entrance to the
building and post yourself there in case there is trouble or
he bursts out the front door to surprise us.

Sid and Carlos walk to the front door while Rooney
positions his men.

Sid cautiously steps into the abandoned warehouse.
It's twilight dark inside, although light pours inside through
the many broken windows. The interior is a combination
of shipping offices, conveyor belts and work stations.
Various types of toys are scattered across the floor and
throughout the building. In the center of the warehouse
is a stairway that leads to the upper floors.

The sound of creaking floorboards from above calls Sid
to creep   toward the stairway,.357 magnum revolver
drawn. He starts to tiptoe up the metal steps. He is

stopped at the end of the flight at the 2nd floor by a stern voice which comes from someplace above. The speaker isn't in sight.

SHOOTER   (out of view - whole conversation)
Far enough

SID
From your actions it seems you want to talk.

SHOOTER
Yeah, I just wanted to let you know you don't have to worry about Maxxus getting killed.

SID
Why not?

SHOOTER
I plan to shoot him for you. I know you really want him. But he won't stay dead for long.

SID
How do you figure that?

SHOOTER
He promised that he'd rise from the dead after only 2 days.

SID
I see. One day less than Jesus.

SHOOTER
Only to show he's here to finish the work of Jesus.

SID
Did Maxxus tell you this himself?

SHOOTER
No, I figured it out from listening to his podcasts.

SID
Was that you who shot at him yesterday?

SHOOTER
Yeah, I was right on target too, but I guess he wasn't ready to die yet. I'm a sharpshooter. Can't miss. Was a top ranked sniper in the military.

SID
What do you mean he wasn't ready to die yet?

SHOOTER
Like I said - I was right on target. The round was heading straight between his eyes. Then... (pauses)

SID
Then?
SHOOTER
The cartridge I fired just vanished. Disappeared into thin air. So I figured that it was Maxxus' doing. He wasn't ready to die and made the shot just vanish.

SID

Maybe you might want to talk to Maxxus before taking any more shots at him. Make sure it's what he really wants. Maybe he changed his mind.

SHOOTER
Me talk to him! Ha! He wouldn't talk to a nobody like me face to face. Anyway - my mission's been set. Can't deviate from it now.

SID
Maybe we could get a message to Maxxus for you.

SHOOTER
No, no message (hesitates). Wait - maybe tell him that it'll be painless. He won't feel a thing.

SID
Maybe we can talk about this. You might not have it all figured out right.

SHOOTER
Naw, I got it all planned. I'm going to…

He is interrupted by the sound of items falling from the unsteady shelves on the first floor.
There is the sound of rapid footsteps as the shooter runs away.
Sid climbs to the second floor and follows the sound of movement but when he reaches the point where it stops finds it was a bowling ball rolled across the floor to draw him in that direction.

Sid scans the second floor but no one is in sight. The shooter escaped by pre-planned route.

Sid exits at the same location where he'd entered. Carlos is still there and tenses as Sid comes out.

CARLOS
What happened?

SID
He had the whole thing planned out. Had some type of secret escape path ready.

CARLOS
Is he some kind of crank?

SID
No, I'd say he's very dangerous ex-military and he's got Maxxus in his gunsites.

CARLOS
What'll we do?

SID
Very little we can do about a crack sharpshooter who knows guerilla tactics and plans to assassinate his target no matter what.

CARLOS
But wouldn't that get Maxxus out of our way?

SID

Wouldn't that make us an accomplice to murder if we did nothing?

CARLOS
Yeah, maybe so.

SID
Tell me, sergeant Montoya, are you as good at search techniques and data collection as I've been told?

CARLOS (confused)
I...uh...yeah, I like to consider myself something of an expert. I know better than most people where things are likely to be hidden for some reason.

SID
Right, just the man. I want you to go to the victim's apartment and dig up anything pertinent that can link Maxxus to Ms. Barges. And find out something about that mystery husband of hers who no one's been able to locate. He might be our sharpshooter here. Pore through everything you can.

CARLOS
Like a sieve.

SID
All right, get going. And keep it kind of secret. Only between us working this case, okay.

CARLOS

Got it.

IMPORTANT DISCOVERY

Inside the Barges' apartment alone, Carlos follows orders and searches with expert skill. Sgt. Montoya methodically picks through everything, including many written documents but finds nothing.

He sits at the laptop in the small office space area and notices that the drawer of the desk it is on seems loose on the front. A little prying reveals that the drawer has a false front. He unscrews it with his pocket knife and a sheet of writing paper drops to the floor.

Montoya picks up the paper and carries it to a table in the small kitchenette where he lays it flat. Written on the top of the paper in bold letters is: MASTER'S WORDS. Below this is a long string of words, only one per line, making up several separate lines. A few lines stand out: CAST OUT FOREVER. ONLY I CAN SAVE YOU. ONLY I KNOW THE TRUTH. DISOBEDIENCE IS NOT AN OPTION. And scrawled quickly in a red lipstick at the bottom of the pages are these 4 numbers...4158 or 4153. The last number is difficult to see.

He takes several photographs of the paper by his mobile phone and forwards copies of the picture to both Risa and Sid, no one else. He then folds the paper, puts it inside a coat pocket, refastens the front to the drawer, then departs.

MEETING WITH DESI

Risa returns the next evening to the back office/studio where Maxxus does his podcasts and sits in one of the chairs facing the viewing screen alone. Risa peeks up with annoyance at the screen on which Maxxus is spewing his latest podcast.

A peculiar, hypnotic music plays behind him as Maxxus raves.

MAXXUS (on screen)
No matter the affliction, the real problem is that we are all victims of the ruling class of billionaires, oligarchs and pedophiles. I will fight for you - for us. Using the strength of the masses behind me. I will make life better for you also with the god light that has been given to me and will keep us on our destined path,the one that leads us all to prosperity, love and liberty. I will make every day great.

Risa is interrupted as the receptionist enters the office. She uses a handheld device to mute the screen. Her name is DESI RICHARDSON. She is about 21 years of age, thin, blonde, very pretty and the giggly type but also friendly and deceptively savvy.

DESI (to Risa)
Oh, you're here. I didn't' see you come in.

RISA
You were away from your desk when I entered. I have a dinner date with Maxxus and thought I'd show up a little early.

DESI
That's fine. I could use the company in this gloomy place. It gets lonely here - not many visitors.

RISA
Sure.

DESI
I check here in the back room now and then to see if he has any...visitors.

RISA
By visitors do you mean female visitors only?

DESI
Yeah, they throw themselves at him. Not just the sex; he claims he's filling them with God presence.

RISA
I'm not one of those. I'm applying for Ms Barges' job.

DESI
It is sad what happened to her. Poor kid.

RISA
Do you have any idea why she'd kill herself?

DESI
Not really. Although, she did seem out of sorts during her last week here.

RISA
Do you know why?

DESI
Not really. She was here with Max from the beginning. A real believer. Then all of a sudden she wasn't.

RISA
How long have you worked here?

DESI
About 5 years.

RISA
Are you one of his devoted followers?

DESI
(makes a face)
Hardly. I don't really listen to any of his rantings. In fact, I always put in ear plugs when he's on.

Desi motions toward the set of ear plugs strung across her shoulders.

RISA
Were Debbie and Maxxus close?

DESI
I don't think in a romantic way. But they were kind of like partners till the falling out.

RISA
What was that about?

DESI
I don't know for sure. Just that Debbie seemed to suddenly lose all interest in the movement. She was a real fanatic for a long time. One of his first followers.

RISA
I see.

DESI
One thing comes to mind though.

RISA
Oh?

DESI
About 2 weeks ago Debbie made an unauthorized visit to his podcast booth up there. (points to studio and grimaces) Where Max keeps all of his data.

RISA
No one but him is allowed in there?

DESI
(emphatically)
No, mam! He was furious when Debbie used the special door code to get in there one day while he was...entertaining...a woman at his Beverley Hills mansion.

RISA
There's a code?

DESI
An alarm goes off if the door to the booth is opened without the code.

RISA
You don't have that code do you?

DESI
(emphatically)
No, mam! I don't want to know it either. I really just work here. I don't care what he's up to. Although, I do get paid pretty well to just mind my own business.

RISA
Nothing wrong with that. Tell me…

Interruption. The television screen on the wall goes dark.

DESI
Sorry... He's finished with the rant and will be coming out any second. I sure don't want him to see me with these ear buds.

The door to the raised studio opens and Desi quickly stuffs her ear buds into a pocket and scurries out of the room.

Maxxus closes the door behind him and marches down the ramp from the studio like a conquering hero.

MAXXUS (to Risa)
I see you're here a little early. Can't resist?

RISA
I got hungry early.

MAXXUS
(stands over her)
What did you think of my last podcast?

RISA
Powerful I guess is the word.

MAXXUS
I prefer - glorious, impressive! Have to get their attention to gain their loyalty.

RISA
To what end? I'm still hazy about your ultimate goal.

MAXXUS
(grinning)
To take over the world, of course.

RISA
Your following isn't quite large enough.

MAXXUS
Not yet. But that's what you're here for.

RISA
Sounds like I'm hired.

MAXXUS
On probation. Let's see how you handle what will happen tonight. You do have some pretty impressive credentials. I checked.

RISA
I already told you that.

MAXXUS
Come on. Let's go to dinner. Doing podcasts like the last one leaves me ravenous.

They leave the room. And on this meeting Risa envisions Maxxus as an articulate, cultured date with the appearance to match. Not quite her initial view of him.

A FLAMING EXIT

One of the most famous and busiest restaurants in Los Angeles, Crossings Kitchen. Tonight it is crowded with people as usual, but Maxxus and Risa have only to appear and they are led to his reserved table in the center of the large room. A waiter brings them menus and a designated waterboy fills their water glasses.

MAXXUS
I chose this table intentionally.

RISA
You have unusual tastes, then. Most people don't like to be seated in the middle of a crowd.

MAXXUS
It was a tactical choice tonight.

RISA
Quick escape later, maybe? Dine and Dash.

MAXXUS (smirking)
Ha, in an odd sort of way…maybe so.

RISA
But wouldn't a table near the exit be better for that?

MAXXUS

You will see.

RISA
Okay.

MAXXUS
But don't worry - I do expect something extraordinary to happen to me here tonight.

RISA
Then am I to consider this as my first assignment as your new PR person?

MAXXUS
Yes, yes that's a good way to phrase it.

RISA
I'm good at coming up with phrases. That's my business.

MAXXUS
After tonight you may have to come up with ones you've never used before.

RISA
Since I apparently have been hired, can I inquire as to salary?

MAXXUS
Prepare a reasonable figure - meaning below 1 million a year - and leave the number with the receptionist. I'll honor it.

RISA
One thing I don't joke about is money. Now…
MAXXUS
One thing I don't possess is a sense of humor.

RISA
This job is sounding better than I expected.

MAXXUS
Speaking of expectations: I'll expect a lot from you. Starting tonight. The world is a large place to conquer.

RISA
And the battle starts here?

MAXXUS
Look around. One of the fanciest restaurants in LA. Crowded on at the peak hour with the most influential people. As good a place to start as any.

RISA
So, these important, well-connected people are going to witness some kind of event and…

MAXXUS
(interrupts)
…brag that they were here on the night it happened.

RISA
You may be the most egotistical person I have ever met.

MAXXUS

Humility only gets in the way.

RISA
(shaking the menu)
Not very humble fare here.

MAXXUS
Yes, let the hoi polloi eat cake.

RISA
Or grass, as King Louis's finance minister suggested.

They begin to study their menus.

They order, dine, then discuss matters with coffee.

RISA
Can I ask you about Debbie, my predecessor?

MAXXUS
As long as you keep it civil.
RISA

Civil? What do you mean?

MAXXUS
You remember I was called in for questioning about her
death by the LAPD?

RISA
Yes. You told me. A good chance at publicity got away.

MAXXUS

Yes. But the questioning bordered on defamatory. Like about the child.

RISA
Child?

MAXXUS
Didn't you know that Debbie had a child? Little boy about 3 or 4 years old.

RISA
(hesitating)
No, I didn't know about him.

MAXXUS
And that her husband had run off on her about a year ago? And she lost interest in the...group.

RISA
That's something I don't know about.

MAXXUS
Anyway, the police made it seem like I had something to do with that - the child and her husband running off - and seemed to be trying to make a case out of it.

RISA
That's what police do.

MAXXUS
No to me they don't.

RISA
I hope you didn't tell them anything. You're right, they will make up their own evidence.

Maxxus peers forcefully toward Risa. His stare wields so much force that she drops her coffee cup down onto the saucer.

MAXXUS
(deep voice)
So, what is it you want to ask about Debbie?

RISA
(slightly dazed)
Whatever it was - it isn't important.

MAXXUS
Ah, I've chosen you well.

RISA
(head clearing)
Meaning what?

MAXXUS
You have a good effect on me. Electrifying my basic animal instincts.

RISA
You're not going to bite me are you?

MAXXUS

(roars with laughter)
Ha - no, but I suggest you back your chair away from the table a couple of inches.

As Risa does as instructed, Maxxus motions for more water to be brought to the table. When the boy arrives with a pitcher of water, Maxxus grabs it from his hands and lays it on Risa's side of the table. With the water boy remaining, Maxxus then summons the waiter who comes and stands beside the water boy.

MAXXUS (to Risa)
Watch and note what happens.

Maxxus then uses his chair as a step stool and climbs onto the table top, drawing the attention of the entire room. He then gestures with gusto toward Risa.

MAXXUS
(shouting)
Everyone observe! I am Maxxus. You are about to witness a miracle. Do not blink. I will rise again with an important prophecy in 2 days. Pose any questions to the woman at this table, my publicist.

Maxxus then drops his arms to his sides and disappears in a ball of flame. Chaos erupts amid Risa who leaps from her chair in shock.

SIFTING THE ASHES

Groups of diners gather around the table where the event occurred. A waiter approaches Risa who is still standing at her seat, shocked.

WAITER
You are Risa, ma'am?

RISA
Yes.

WAITER
You have a phone call at the reservation desk. If you'd follow me.

The 2 wind their way through the milling crowd to the reservation desk where Risa is handed a landline phone receiver.

RISA
Hello? Who's this?

MAXXUS
Who do you think?

RISA
Where are you?

MAXXUS

Dead. But I'll rise again to life in 2 days at the end of Santa Monica pier with a prophecy for the world. Spread that story to everyone.

Maxxus hangs up. So does Risa. She then returns to her table just as police stream into the restaurant to control the situation. Last among them is Lt. Myers who joins Risa at the scene of the disturbance.

RISA
How'd you know I was here?

SID
We're tracking you.

RISA
(uncertain)
I guess that's good.

SID
Looks like we can stop tracking you now since Maxxus seems to have imploded.

RISA
He's not quite gone. I just got a phone call from him. Took it at the reservation desk. Said he'd return in 2 days.

SID
Smart guy. Didn't use a mobile phone because it could be traced.

Ted Friedman joins the 2 from the crowd of diners, wearing civilian attire.

RISA
(surprise)
Dr. Ted. What're you doing here?

DR. FRIEDMAN
I take my wife out for fine dining once in a while. I sent her home. Too much smoke around here.

RISA
I'm starting to feel stalked.

DR. FRIEDMAN
My interest is in Maxxus. I was waiting or wondering when he'd pull off a stunt like this.

RISA
Stunt? What do you mean?

DR. FRIEDMAN
Something shocking but harmless to get himself noticed by the general public.

SID
Let's take a closer look at this tabletop.
The 3 gather around the table. A scorch spot is left at the location where Maxxus was standing and a 4 inch high pile of fine, brown ashes is in the center of it.

SID (to Ted)
What do you make of it Doc. Some kind of trick, then?

DR. FRIEDMAN
Not a common trick at any rate. If it had been a common magician's illusion there wouldn't be any sign of burning or any residue left on the table like that pile of ashes.

SID
Explain.

DR. FRIEDMAN
Well, a common trick is pre-planned operation and as such artificial. There would be no need for scorch marks or the residue of ashes to convince the viewer that the subject had vanished. They would see him disappear with their own eyes.

SID
Continue, please.

DR. FRIEDMAN
The scorch mark is proof of intense heat. And the pile of ashes is a sign that something was incinerated here. Those may be human ashes.

RISA
What!

SID
I assumed the ashes were from the table cloth.

DR. FRIEDMAN

Have you ever known burned cloth to leave this volume and type of material?

SID
No. We'll have it analyzed at the lab. Then we'll know more.

RISA
But if these ashes are human they can't belong to Maxxus. He isn't dead. I just talked to him.

SID
Can you be sure it wasn't a recorded message?

RISA
Pretty sure. Someone would have to have sent it. And I doubt his receptionist would.

SID
No, it doesn't seem likely he was consumed by this fire. Smell the tabletop.

DR. FRIEDMAN
Right.   No smell of gasoline, kerosene or any other accelerant I can think of.

RISA
What about alcohol? There's plenty of that around here.

SID

No. Not nearly a powerful enough accelerant to consume an entire human body.

DR. FRIEDMAN
That's assuming he was consumed.

SID
What're you thinking, Doc?

DR. FRIEDMAN
I think that he disappeared all right but not necessarily being consumed by flames. He just wanted to create that illusion.

SID
Then it was a trick?

DR. FRIEDMAN
No, I don't think so.

SID
You're really confusing me now, Doc.

RISA
Me, too.

SID (to Risa)
Risa, you were closest to the scene. Tell us exactly what happened just before Maxxus vanished.

RISA
He called the water boy over and asked for a pitcher of water.

SID
A pitcher? A little unusual, huh?

RISA
Then he called another waiter over for some reason and he stood next to the water boy. Next thing, Max climbed onto the tabletop.

SID
Okay, then.

RISA
He announced who he was, and to expect something amazing to happen. Then he shouted to the room to look toward me and to contact me if they had any questions.

SID
Basic misdirection. These are all the moves a magician makes to distract his audience. And, I'd guess he added the waiter and water boy so that it would be easier for him to mix in with them when making his escape. A basic magician's M.O.

RISA
Finally, at the end, he threw his arms at his side and vanished in a burst of flames.

SID

What color was the fire?

RISA
Color? Uh, it was a type of bluish green I think.

DR. FRIEDMAN
I see what you're getting at Lieutenant Myers. If it had been human combustion the flames would have been most likely yellow or orange.

SID
Yes, this sounds more like a type of chemical fire.

RISA
So what does that tell us?

SID
Have you ever seen the flames that accompany a pile of magazines being burned? What color are they?

RISA
(haltingly)
Kind of bluish...green.

SID
Implying that maybe some form of oversized poster or other similar image was set ablaze here?
RISA
That still doesn't account for how Maxxus disappeared.

DR. FRIEDMAN

True. He just wanted to make a big show of his disappearance. Like spontaneous human combustion. But he in fact did vanish.

SID
Do you mean like to sneak off unnoticed?

DR. FRIEDMAN
No, I mean vanished. Bilocated to another spot.

SID
You're losing me again, Doc.

DR. FRIEDMAN
As we have been saying all along: this man has unusual powers beyond the normal human being. He reminds me of some rare cases I studied in old, obscure medical journals. But I can't be sure yet.

SID
Sure of what? That Maxxus is some kind of super human?

DR. FRIEDMAN
We'll know a lot more once we get these ashes examined at the lab.

SID
Okay, Doc. With Maxxus out of sight for awhile he'll have to stay that way until his predicted return. This might give

Risa a good chance to do some investigating at his podcast studio.

RISA
Right.

DR. FRIEDMAN
But be extra-cautious.

RISA
Yeah, I think earlier tonight he tried to trick me. He asked me things about Mrs. Barges' life which were not correct and wanted to see if I'd correct him on them. I didn't slip up though.

SID
Right. I'd be surprised if he didn't try something like that.

DR. FRIEDMAN
Speaking of which: I think we better break this up. It's getting a little long for us to be questioning a supposed witness.

SID
You're right. Maxxus might have followers right here tonight who might get suspicious. Who knows, even members of the force.

The 3 break apart and Sid goes on to question other witnesses to the disturbance.

Early next morning Ted and Sid visit the LAPD lab where they discuss results on tests made on the ashes from the restaurant with HERNAN ALVAREZ. Hernan is a tall, thin chemist in his late 20's. The 3 stand by a long counter on which are 3 piles of ashes of the same size and consistency, side by side.

HERNAN
Would you care to examine the 3 samples of ashes on the counter?

SID
I assume that at least 1 of them is from the disturbance at the restaurant last night?

HERNAN
Yes. Can you determine which of the 3 it is?

Three small wooden tongue depressors are laid out on the counter for their use.

HERNAN
You can use the tongue depressors to probe the material if you like. None of it is toxic.

Sid and Ted both probe and then smell the 3 lumps of ashes.

HERNAN

Any idea which of the 3 might be evidence from the restaurant?

Sid points to the one in the center.

HERNAN
Why did you choose that one?

SID
Because it's the worst smelling of the lot.

HERNAN
Astute observation. Humans are noticeable by their particularly rank odor.

DR. FRIEDMAN
Then those are human ashes?

HERNAN
Uncertain. We can't currently differentiate the ashes of higher mammals from one another.

DR. FRIEDMAN
But then why the remark about the bad odor?

HERNAN
Logically, that would be a proper way to differentiate human ashes from those of other mammals.

SID
To which mammals do the ashes on the ends belong?
HERNAN

The one on the left is from a dog. The right is from a cow. The middle one may be from a human or a pig I would suggest, but can't be definite.

SID
(snorting)
Fine company, pairing a human and a pig.

DR. FRIEDMAN
I don't think the pigs of the world would take offense.

HERNAN
Well, we are closer related than most people care to admit. I can't speak for the pigs' opinion though.

Hernan motions the 2 men over to a large microscope at the end of the counter.

HERNAN
You may find very interesting what I found in deeper examination of the ashes from the center sample. Have a look.

Sid and Ted peer through the microscope. What they see are specks of colorless material spread throughout the ashes.

SID (to Hernan)
What do you make of it?

HERNAN
Bits of Micro-plastic. I suspect that some type of container held the contents that became ashes and both were consumed by the fire.

DR. FRIEDMAN
(exclaims)
Shit!

HERNAN
An inspired observation, doctor. That may exactly be what the ashes represent.

SID
What!

HERNAN
Feces. That would account for the small sample size of the ashes. An entire human body would have produced far more material. But a small sample from a body, well…

SID
So the ashes may or may not be a gift from Maxxus he left behind.

DR. FRIEDMAN
It would be in keeping with his view of other lowly human beings. So, one fact remains. Maxxus did plan to vanish in a ball of flame and made it not look like a magician's trick. I repeat: made it NOT look like a trick!

SID
What're you implying?

DR. FRIEDMAN
He vanished and it wasn't a trick.

SID
You mean he could perform genuine magic - like Merlin or the like!

DR. FRIEDMAN
I told you that you'd think I was crazy.

SID
I am starting to wonder, Doc.

DR. FRIEDMAN
Let's finish this in my office. Maybe I can convince you of my sanity with some medical evidence.

Both men thank Hernan, then depart.

MAGICAL POWERS

Sid and Ted resumed their conversation in the doctor's office. They sit across from each other at the desk.

DR. FRIEDMAN
I believe we are fortunate - or unfortunate - enough to be witnessing a genuine case of accelerated pseudologia fantastica.

SID
Which is?

DR. FRIEDMAN
In its base form it's pathological lying which is so potent that the subject believes his own falsehoods and can convince others the same.

SID
Yes, I've dealt with a few of those in my 26 years here.

DR. FRIEDMAN
Not like this case. A person with such an elevated IQ as Maxxus will be able to make whatever he creates in his mind seem real to everyone. He can give reality to his lies.

SID
That's kind of hard to believe, Doc.

DR. FRIEDMAN
It isn't a common condition. In fact, I've only found 2 cases on record of this type of advanced condition. One occurred in the early 19th century, the other in the mid 17th century. Records before then become pretty scarce.

SID
What happened in the first case you studied?

DR. FRIEDMAN
The first subject exhibited a type of hyper Munchausen syndrome. It's a type of hypochondria.

SID
Yes, I've heard of it.

DR. FRIEDMAN
But in this particular case it was of such a highly developed nature that the subject could convince medical practitioners beyond doubt that he was suffering from whatever ailment he chose to describe. He was able to mentally either cause their testing devices to correspond with the results he desired or else he could have caused his body to temporarily actually develop the chosen symptoms.

SID
How does that relate to our case?

DR. FRIEDMAN

You'll see. But in the case I just mentioned, by using these mental powers the subject was able to prove that he could not have committed the serial killings that the authorities expected him of performing.

SID
I see. And your next example?

DR. FRIEDMAN
Even more striking. A subject wanted for murder hung himself before the law could get him.

SID
Guilt?

DR. FRIEDMAN
Hardly. It was his escape. These type do not have consciences so they never experience guilt.

SID
So what was the point in hanging himself?

DR. FRIEDMAN
Like I said: to escape punishment. In a letter he left with a close friend he advised her not to worry and that he'd meet her later after the fake hanging.

SID
Fake hanging? How did he manage that?

DR. FRIEDMAN
Earlier he'd also proven his ability to convince medical practitioners of a severe illness he didn't really have. Like the previous case. However, on this occasion he was clearly guilty but planned to escape the consequence by committing suicide of a type.

SID
Of a type?

DR. FRIEDMAN
With his suicide by hanging, he planned to stop all bodily functions to fool authorities into thinking he was really dead.

SID
Something went wrong?

DR. FRIEDMAN
Yes, he proved to be too thorough of a hangman and his act was so well conceived that he ended up breaking his neck for real.

SID
And do you think that Maxxus has these types of... powers?

DR. FRIEDMAN
I'm almost certain of it.

SID

(thoughtfully)
Impersonating God, huh?

DR. FRIEDMAN
You might say that. Yes.

SID
Well, that would explain one weird event. I had a clandestine meeting with the gunman who took a shot at Maxxus after we questioned him the other day.

DR. FRIEDMAN
Yes. And?

SID
The gunman claimed to be a sharpshooter. And he swears that his shot was right on target and should have killed Maxxus. He was right on the mark.

DR. FRIEDMAN
Then why didn't the bullet kill him?

SID
The gunman said that the cartridge vanished into thin air inches from striking the target. He also said that he wants to kill Maxxus to see him rise again from the dead.

DR. FRIEDMAN
Sure Maxxus has a messianic complex as well.

SID

So do you think that Maxxus actually vanished in a burst of flames last night at the restaurant?

DR. FRIEDMAN
You've heard of the swamis of India and other holy men - even Christian saints - who can bilocate?

SID
Yes, but...he's no saint or holy man.

DR. FRIEDMAN
So? He thinks he is. And being a saint isn't necessary. Look at Rasputin. He was hardly holy. And there is the almighty power of pure evil to consider.

SID
Okay. All of this is interesting, but where is Maxxus now. He has certainly disappeared in one way or another.

DR. FRIEDMAN
I guess he's laying low until his grand reappearance on Santa Monica Pier.

SID
While all the television networks and news outlets are going wild about the sudden disappearance of the world's most listened-to podcaster in a burst of fire. They'll all be covering his return at the pier.

KNOCK ON DOOR

DR. FRIEDMAN
Enter.

CARLOS
(enters)
I've been looking all over for you Detective Myers.

SID
Well this is a police precinct and I am a police Lieutenant who works here.

CARLOS
Yes, but you have been traveling all over the building.

SID
What have you got for me, sergeant?

CARLOS
I gathered some really important evidence that was hidden in the Borges apartment.

SID
Ha, I knew you'd come up with something.

Sgt. Montoya hands Sid the paper he found at the desk in the apartment. Sid lies it on the desk and both he and Ted bend forward to examine it.

SID
(reading paper)
Verbal control phrases and some type of number code.

DR. FRIEDMAN

I wonder what those numbers unlock?

CARLOS
I took photos of this on site and sent them to the Lieutenant and Risa.

Sid and Ted stare gravely at each other.

SID
(moans)
Risa, too?

CARLOS
(nervously)
Uh, yes. Did I do something wrong?

SID
We keep communication with her at a bare minimum because she's under cover. Anyone could pick up her phone and read that message.

CARLOS
But last night at the restaurant. You did interview her there, didn't you? Wasn't that in full view?

SID
Perfectly proper. She was a first hand witness to a public disturbance and it would've been unusual for her not to be questioned.

DR. FRIEDMAN

Nothing we can do about it now. We can only hope she's the only one who saw the message and immediately erased it.

KNOCK ON DOOR

DR. FRIEDMAN
Enter.

A uniformed officer comes inside. He hands a folder to Lt. Myers.

OFFICER 2
And...there's someone here to see you. A military man. Says it's about the medallion that was found at the murder scene.

Myers stands, pats Montoya on the shoulder.

SID
Care to join me, Sergeant and find out what this is all about? These military men always make me uneasy.

CARLOS
Sure, Lieutenant.

Myers, Montoya and the uniformed officer exit the office.

MILITARY INVOLVEMENT

Myers and Montoya enter the Lieutenant's office and a MEDIUM SIZED, MUSCULAR MAN IN INFANTRY MILITARY UNIFORM, CAPTAIN PAUL SIMMONS, rises to attention from the chair before the desk.

SID
(smiling)
As you were Captain.

The captain removes hat and returns to his seat.

CAPTAIN SIMMONS
Sir.

Sid sits behind the desk and Sgt. Montoya takes a chair to the side.

SID
We don't often get visits from men in the military, Captain. At least, not since the invasion of Los Angeles in 2025.

CAPTAIN SIMMONS
I assure you that the invasion, as you call it, was not a personal choice. Not even my department.

SID
So, what brings you here today?

CAPTAIN SIMMONS

It seems that your investigators may have located the whereabouts of one of our missing personnel.

SID
What makes you think so?

The captain removes a medallion from an inner coat pocket and places it on the desk. It is the same type that Lt. Myers removed from the dead Mrs. Barges' clutches.

SID
Yes, we found a medallion just like that in the hands of a murder victim.

CAPTAIN SIMMONS
It's a very special piece which only a few men in my division have ever carried.

SID
Which division might that be?

CAPTAIN SIMMONS
Clandestine operations. Performing expedient assassinations along with other activities in foreign lands. That's all I am allowed to say.

SID
That seems sufficient. And what led you to our precinct in this matter?

CAPTAIN SIMMONS

Someone from your precinct was engaged in a particularly tenacious investigation into its identity and its place of origin.

Myers motions to Montoya who nods.

SID
That person would be Sergeant Carlos Montoya. Good man. Thorough. He is a tenacious investigator.

CAPTAIN SIMMONS
As I mentioned, we are a clandestine division which normally does not look favorably upon outside contact. But in this case you may have done us a service.

SID
How so?

CAPTAIN SIMMONS
One of our operatives in the Taiwan theatre had gone missing about a decade ago and we'd never been able to determine what happened to him or trace his current whereabouts. We...uh...don't like that.

SID
That's very...interesting. Can you give us his name, description, etcetera?

CAPTAIN SIMMONS

I obviously cannot give you his identity. But I can give a physical description. Right now he would be about 40 - 45 years of age, about six foot two, powerful build, full head of dark hair, erratic of behavior, extreme intelligence, possibly subject to fits of derangement.

CARLOS
(shock)
That sounds like...

SID
(cuts him off)
I think Dr. Friedman should be in on this.

Myers activates inter office intercom.

SID
Ted, come into my office, will you?

DR. FRIEDMAN
Be right there.

CAPTAIN SIMMONS (to Sid)
You seem to have some idea as to who this person is?

SID
Possibly. We'll know more in a moment. I've called in Dr. Ted Friedman - our ranking clinical psychologist.

Dr. Friedman enters and stands beside Sid's desk.

SID (to Ted)

Ted, this is Captain Simmons. He's looking for a person who fits this description: about 40 - 45 years of age, about six foot two, powerful build, full head of dark hair, erratic of behavior, extreme intelligence, possibly subject to fits of derangement.

DR. FRIEDMAN
Maxxus?

CAPTAIN SIMMONS
Who?

SID
He's currently a suspect in a murder investigation.

DR. FRIEDMAN
Captain Simmons, would you happen to know if the person you're looking for has been diagnosed with any serious form of brain disease?

CAPTAIN SIMMONS
I cannot say precisely, however, in his final days with the division he showed signs of some form of severe psychological impairment.

DR. FRIEDMAN (to Myers)
Possibly organic brain syndrome.

SID (to captain Simmons)
If this is the man you are looking for, he is currently a highly prominent podcaster with a following in the millions. How is it even possible that none of your personnel would've noticed him?

CAPTAIN SIMMONS
My division is secured strictly to the Taiwan theatre of operations and would have very little communication with the outside world.

SID
But our subject must have a military record and background.

CAPTAIN SIMMONS
No, sir. Officially, he does not exist. And this, Maxxus, as you call him, has an astonishing skill of impersonation.

SID
What is your intention insofar as his disposition: do you want him placed in your custody?

CAPTAIN SIMMONS
No. The only thing we seek is a definite identification. Our only and sole purpose is to make certain that he has not gone over to the other side. Remember, as a person he does not in reality exist.

CARLOS
(interjecting)
Which explains why we couldn't locate any background details at all about Maxxus.

CAPTAIN SIMMONS

Nor do we possess any. I assure you, he has no official identity.

SID
Well Captain Simmons, I'd say we probably have identified your man.

CAPTAIN SIMMONS
Do you know his current whereabouts?

SID
Before I answer that: you don't happen to have a sniper assigned to assassinate him do you?

CAPTAIN SIMMONS
Why would you suggest that?

SID
Because there is someone out there with a rifle trying to shoot him. And, I'm not a complete moron.

CAPTAIN SIMMONS
I can assure you that he is not under our orders.

SID
Good to know. And as to the whereabouts of Maxxus: he vanished from a local dining establishment in a burst of flame last night.

CAPTAIN SIMMONS

He, uh...what!

SID
Don't tell me you haven't seen that story about the disappearing diner that's been all over the news?
CAPTAIN SIMMONS
Oh, so that's him! Yeah, it sounds like something a person of his abilities would do.

SID
He's due to reappear among us at the end of Santa Monica Pier. If you care to see him in the flesh, that might be the place to do it. But don't plan to take him. I have a personal score to settle with him.

Sid pats his suit coat on the location where he keeps the Barges woman's suicide note.

CAPTAIN SIMMONS
I would imagine that many people do.

SID
Would one of them be the husband of the murdered woman whose death we're investigating?

CAPTAIN SIMMONS
One would think so.

SID
Maybe you can help us now on that matter, Captain.

CAPTAIN SIMMONS
How so?

SID
The only lead we have on the identity of her husband is that he's in the military and is assigned to Germany.

CAPTAIN SIMMONS
That would be unusual.

SID
What is unusual is that we can find no information at all about his identity.

CAPTAIN SIMMONS
I assume you checked military records.

SID
That was the first place we tried. There are no records matching this individual.

CAPTAIN SIMMONS
But how can I help?

SID
Tell me this - how do you think that the specialized medallion that was in the dead woman's hand came to be there? I mean - how would she have such a rare item?

CAPTAIN SIMMONS
(emits a loud hmmm)

One way she could've gotten it would've been directly from the owner of it, of course.

SID
Is it possible that Maxxus, the murderer, the victim's husband and the person you're seeking are all the same person?

CAPTAIN SIMMONS
(nodding slowly)
But if he were married to the victim wouldn't there be records of that?

SID
Sure, if the marriage was legal. Maybe they just lived together and called themselves husband and wife.

CAPTAIN SIMMONS
That's certainly been done before.

SID
Well, Captain, I'm really glad you paid us a visit. You have solved a lot of mysteries for us.

CAPTAIN SIMMONS
And as far as the military is concerned, you may handle your suspect in any way you see fit.

Sid slowly walks toward the window and speaks low to himself as he peers out onto the LA street.

SID (to self)
Ha, so the great Maxxus is a deserter.

TRAPPED

Risa uses a skeleton key provided by the Department, Risa to break into the outer office of Maxxus's office. It is dark and vacant inside due to the early hour.

Risa flicks on the lights and heads into the back office area which is also vacant. She walks up the short ramp to the vault-like podcast chamber and faces the electronic box that operates the alarm system to the studio door. She then takes from her purse her phone and looks at the photo of the code to the door that Detective Montoya sent her.

RISA (to self)
(reading)
Let's see - 4..1..5 or 8 or maybe 3. The last number is a 3 or an 8.

She punches in the numbers on the panel. 4...1...5...she hovers her finger over the 3, then at the last minute moves it to 8 and presses. A slight click and the light on the panel goes from red to green.

Risa then uses the same skeleton key to open the Studio door. It's a bunked type of heavily sealed room. On one side the walls are lined with electronic apparatus. Opposite is the large desk and leather chair from which Maxxus performs his podcasts. At the end of the room is a large, three sectioned heavy filing cabinet which seems like a barricade. The room comes into better view when Risa turns on the overhead lighting. She then wanders inside as if caught in a trance, the room is so overpowering.

A loud voice from behind awakens her, sounding like a chainsaw in the silence.

MAXXUS
So you've entered my lair without permission to learn my secrets.

Risa spins to see the hulking figure of Maxxus, appearing more monster than man, blocking her path to escape.

RISA
Did you expect me not to come in here?

MAXXUS
You have a very confusing speech pattern. But to reply to your strangely phrased question: then you being in here is only because of unbounded enthusiasm?

RISA
You might say that.

MAXXUS
I might. And I might even be partially correct. But what is the real cause of your enthusiasm?

RISA
Why ask? You do seem to have all the answers.

MAXXUS
Even the most careful of us make mistakes. Even you.

RISA
I make as many as the next person.

MAXXUS
Your worst one was underestimating me. Didn't you consider that once I had your mobile phone number that I could forward all of your calls to me?

RISA
You saw the photo sent to me by Montoya?

MAXXUS
A clumsy mistake.

RISA
I'll have to berate him for that.

MAXXUS

You won't have the chance.

RISA
I'm supposed to commit suicide, like Debbie?

MAXXUS
No, that would be too suspicious. An accident would be more believable.

RISA
I don't know. That might look a little suspicious, too.

MAXXUS
No matter. It's a chance I'll take.

RISA
What kind of accident will I have?

MAXXUS
You're going to lock yourself in here and die of suffocation. The walls are impenetrable and soundproof and the door is like that of a bank vault.

RISA
Someone will come looking for me.

MAXXUS
I doubt they'd get here in time. This little bunker has only air for about 4 hours once the filtration system is turned off, which it will be.

RISA
Okay then, assuming I have no hope of escape, can we play this like an old time detective movie?

MAXXUS
What do you mean?

RISA
Tell me the secret of how you converted so many people to your cause so quickly.

MAXXUS
You know, I'd like to tell someone. So someone knows of my greatness. Debbie pretty much figured out what I was doing but still didn't know my process.

RISA
You couldn't take the risk she'd find out so you caused her suicide.

MAXXUS
Who would've thought she had such a weak mind? She responded to a command to commit suicide that I sent her in an email.

RISA
It's pretty clear that you use some type of hypnotic command phrases over your followers but how are the prompts delivered to them?

MAXXUS
I've advanced far beyond basic subliminal commands. The control words I use - as on the paper the other detective found - are electronically destabilized and then reformulated into infrasound pulses in a process of neurotransmission that interacts directly with the subject's cerebral cortex. It's my own creation.

RISA
I still don't quite understand.

MAXXUS
I am surprised! According to your credentials you are trained in the micro integration of inharmonic variants with neural response. Or was that all phony?

RISA
No, my credentials are genuine. But I've never experienced an application as complex as yours.

MAXXUS
(sinister laugh)
Because I alone created it. It operates the same way that used to be called machine language was in former periods of programming when the directions to the operating system were written in technical language which the computer could directly translate without needing a server to interpret them. Like APL - A Programming Language.

RISA

And you use the human brain as a computer and developed a language you could insert directly into it.

MAXXUS
(excitedly)
Yes! Yes! The subject is given infrasound commands which he cannot hear but which penetrate to the subconscious through the neural network!

RISA
My God! That is more than brilliant.

MAXXUS
Quite right. Godlike you might say. It's really unfortunate that you betrayed me like Judas betrayed Christ. You do seem to understand how my conversion process works.

RISA
Too bad the process has been used for such evil intent.

MAXXUS
Evil? Once I'm in control I'll make all things right again. The world will be a safer, secure place under my control.

RISA
I've heard that before.

Maxxus lunges forward for her purse and yanks it from her grasp.

MAXXUS
I have to make sure you don't have a weapon.

He rifles through her pocketbook. There is no weapon but Maxxus comes full face with the "pinwheel" type toy Risa always carries with her. Due to his suffering from organic brain syndrome he is struck with a powerful dizziness and falls to his left.

Risa spurts past him on his right, bursts out the door, but slams directly into an unawares Desi who is just then climbing up the ramp. They collide and entangle. Maxxus storms out of the studio, grabs both women and bodily hurls them inside the small, enclosed room. He slams tight the door, locks it, then turns off all power to the small enclosed room. Laughing, he departs.

Both Desi and Risa use the flashlight option on their mobile phones for illumination.

DESI
I was afraid I'd get locked in here someday.

RISA
Well, this is that day.

DESI
That's why I came prepared.

RISA
Did you bring an extra supply of air? We're going to need it.

DESI

No, but I might have brought us a way out of here.

Desi fishes around in her purse and takes out a tuning fork.

DESI (cont.)
It's a gift from my boyfriend Ricardo - a journeyman electrician - with instructions to tap it on the studio door until the correct tone is made that will open it.

RISA
Maybe we should just call for help on our phones.
DESI
Won't work. Signals can't get out of this tomb.

RISA
I don't think what you're doing will work either. The electricity to the door has been turned off.

DESI
No! That's just it. The system that operates the door works on its own energy. It has to stay on because if it was turned off an alarm would sound, warning that someone had turned it off.

RISA
Oh, I see. Makes sense. Start tapping then.

Desi taps the tuning fork on the metallic inside of the door. There is no response. She attempts different tones, but still no success, Scene concludes with this ongoing process.

STILL TRAPPED

Risa and Desi are still trapped in the broadcast booth. Much time has passed. Both women are deflated from the loss of air and the heat. Desi is still weakly intermittently tapping the door with her tuning fork to no result.

RISA
(shouts with sudden revelation)
Wait! Wait! Your idea is sound - pardon the pun - but not the right frequency.

DESI
(confused)
What? Is the lack of air getting to you?

RISA
No, the mobile phone. The ringtones are electronic and should be closer to the frequency the door uses than the tuning fork.

Risa takes her phone, turns volume to high, presses it to the door, and selects the entire library of ringtones on the device. It isn't long before the door clicks open, responding to the ringtone of "Amazing Grace." Desi springs up the side of the wall and clicks on the light switch, bathing the room in sickly whitish luminescent light and rushing cool air from the vents.

RISA (to Desi)
Go to your desk out front and call 911 on the landline. Tell them that Sergeant Risa Sanchez needs immediate assistance and give them our location.

DESI
(surprise)
You're a cop!

RISA
Undercover. Doing surveillance on Maxxus.

DESI
Guess I'll be out of a job then.

RISA
Don't feel too bad. There's a 25 thousand dollar reward for information leading to the arrest of Maxxus. That will go to you.

DESI
Me!

RISA
You. But you better go make that call right away.

RISA

Come back here after you make it. I'm going to need a little more help.

Desi leaves to make the call. Risa studies the various complex electronic devices around her. A moment later Desi returns.

DESI
(scared)
Look, I just want to get out of here. I'm afraid that that monster is going to come back and kill us before the police arrive.

RISA
That won't happen. This is the night he's supposed to reappear on Santa Monica pier. He's most likely heading that way right now.

DESI
Right. But this place still gives me the creeps.

RISA
Yeah, I know. I just need to get into those filing cabinets (pointing). You don't happen to have a key, do you?

DESI
I'm not supposed to, but…

She digs a key from her pocketbook and hands it to Risa.

RISA
(takes key)
Great. Now, if you could post yourself out at your front desk I'd appreciate it. The police will be here any minute. Let them know what's going on here.

DESI
(studying her face in her compact mirror)
Sure, I need a touch up anyway.

RISA
And I think I'll be making an unscheduled podcast in a little while.

DESI
I'll turn on the TV screens.

Desi leaves the studio for the front office, stopping briefly to turn on the large monitor outside the studio. Risa unlocks the filing cabinets and gasps at the many well known names listed as followers of Maxxus as well as another list of enemies of Maxxus. She then studies more closely the electronic instruments and begins learning how they operate.

A SHOOTING ON THE PIER

It is early evening on the beach area beneath Santa Monica Pier. A huge crowd is gathered in the sand at the area near that section of the extension of the pier. The mood is festive. Police on bicycles ride along the nearby paved paths. Some police walk the pier itself. Sid and Sgt. Montoya have positioned themselves on the beach under the pier near its end.

CARLOS
I'm really worried about Sergeant Sanchez. I can't forgive myself for...for…

SID
I'd hoped we'd have heard from her by now. But we could take that as a good sign.

CARLOS
(Nods)
Maybe. But I made a rookie mistake that might cost a fellow officer her life.

SID
Well, Carlos, you are a rookie. You're highly experienced at search and collection of data, but this is a new area for you. If anyone is at fault it's me.

CARLOS
What would you tell yourself then to feel better about it?

SID
That even when mistakes happen we have to have faith in our fellow officers and their ability to extricate

themselves from dangerous situations that they did not anticipate. Faith, Carlos. In your fellow officer. That's what welds partnerships.

CARLOS
Understood.

The once festive crowd suddenly becomes eerily silent. A human figure appears as if from thin air in the dusky evening light standing on a railing of the pier over the beach side area. His arms spread wide.

CARLOS
Maxxus!

SID
What a target!

A gunshot rings out. Sid and Carlos exchange shocked expressions. Maxxus falls from the pier; but he floats more to the beach below than plummets. Sid, Carlos and other police rush to the scene.

SID (to uniformed officers)
Clear the area and cordon off this site.

Uniformed police form a circular cordon around where Maxxus lay. Sid and Carlos rush over to him. Maxxus is still alive, but barely.

MAXXUS (to Sid)
(weakly)

I take solace in that...that in some other universe I still survive.

Maxxus breathes a final breath and turns his face to the side, eyes close. Sid feels for a pulse. There is none. Sid stands up.

SID (to uniforms nearby)
Someone call for the coroner.

CARLOS
What was it that Maxxus said as he died? Strange last words.

They are interrupted by a commotion in the distance. Sid and Carlos force their way through the crowd to find a man with a rifle being forced into custody by a pair of police officers.

SHOOTER (to Sid)
(shouting)
They've got the wrong person! I didn't shoot this guy.

SID (to shooter)
I recognize your voice.

SHOOTER
I was the one you talked to at that warehouse.

SID
Looks like you hit your target this time.

SHOOTER
No, no it couldn't have been me.

SID
The problem is that you're the only one here with a rifle. So, I'm going to have these 2 officers escort you to the station and we'll talk about it there.

Sid motions to the officers who move off with the shooter.

CARLOS
He sure is adamant about not shooting Maxxus.

SID
I don't know. He seems too obvious of an arrest. We'll see.

Montoya points into the near distance.

CARLOS
Ah, here comes the coroner.

SID
Good. The sooner this Maxxus is pronounced dead the better.

Sid's mobile phone rings. He answers. After a short message which only Sid hears he puts his phone away.

SID (to Montoya)

That was about Risa. She's okay. But she needs help now!. You take care of it. She's at Maxxus' podcast studio.

CARLOS
(excited)
Yes, sir!

SID
Appropriate one of the patrol cars and take a couple of uniforms with you.

Montoya rushes off. Sid walks back toward where Maxxus is lying and meets the coroner. When Sid arrives he finds the coroner kneeling beside the body.

SID (to coroner)
Hi, Jason. How dead is he?

CORONER
As a doornail. One gunshot through the head. Seems to be a .357 magnum.

SID
What! Not a rifle?

CORONER
No. Looks like he was shot from behind from close range. But not close enough to have powder burns.

SID

Shot from behind?

CORONER
Yes, the wound in front is actually an exit wound not an entrance wound.

Sid stiffens back in contemplation.

CORONER
What makes you think he was shot by a rifle?

SID
We grabbed a guy on the beach who had a rifle and the shot seemed to come from the beach area not the pier.

CORONER
(standing beside Sid)
These are just the preliminaries. But the weapon used was a handgun and not a rifle. And he was shot from behind.

SID
(sarcastically)
And from behind, too! Ok. Jason, thanks for the new mystery.

CORONER
Either way, I'm sending him in marked DOA.

Coroner motions for his men to approach and remove the body.

DISSOLVING DELUSIONS

Montoya rushes through the front door of Maxxus's office and stops at the front desk where Desi is sitting.

CARLOS
I'm Detective Montoya. Is Risa here?

DESI
(pointing)
Back there in the studio broadcast booth, getting ready to do a podcast.

Montoya nods and rushes into the back room as the 2 officers who'd come with him enter the office. Montoya climbs the ramp and hurries into the studio chamber where Risa is seated in the oversized podcaster's chair. Montoya runs over to her and hugs her as she remains seated.

RISA
(surprise)
Well, detective, what's this all about? I knew we were making plans together, but...

CARLOS
I...uh, was worried about you. I thought the photo I sent you on your mobile phone might've got you into real trouble.

RISA
I'm sorry you were so worried. But Maxxus had been reading the data on my phone all along anyway and already knew who I was.

CARLOS
Oh. You might want to know that he's dead. Was shot on the pier.

RISA
Couldn't happen to a better person. Well, I'm just about to broadcast a podcast which will expose all of his tricks to his supporters so he won't be a martyr.

CARLOS
I'm just glad that you didn't become one...a martyr to the department. Or something like that.

RISA
That's...sweet.

CARLOS
You know how I feel about you, since our days in data collection.

Risa pats his cheek.

RISA
Right now, why don't you take a seat before the monitor in the inner office and see what kind of a podcaster I'd make.

Sgt.Montoya takes a seat alongside the 2 other policemen and Desi before the wall monitor and watches Risa's podcast.

INTERCHANGE BETWEEN RISA IN STUDIO AND ON THE TV SCREEN

RISA
(Interchanging between studio and TV screen)
Hello, my name is Risa and I am Maxxus's new assistant. Due to a situation beyond his control, Maxxus cannot present a podcast at the moment. So I will fill in for him. I am going to present to you information that will shock you and make you re-consider your chosen spiritual and political path.

Risa turns while within the studio and operates a control that starts the usual background tone used by Maxxus in his podcasts.

RISA
You are all of course familiar with this tone; the one used in all of his previous podcasts. Yes, it seems soothing. But it is also hypnotic. You have been lulled into a semi-

conscious state by this engineered sound for years while watching these podcasts. But what you are going to hear next is something hidden beneath the tone and it is the voice of Maxxus which has been previously so disguised so that you could not hear it audibly but it was heard by your subconscious. Also note the sparkly flicks on the background of the screen; they are hypnotic devices.

Risa turns again and operates another control and this starts a stream of command words made in Maxxus's own voice which can now be heard over the hypnotic tone.

MAXXUS
(voice on the TV screen)
You must obey only me. I am your savior. You trust only me. You will believe only me. Only I can make the world right again. You will worship me. You must vote for me in any election. I will save you. Anyone who does not believe me is an enemy. I am your master.

Rise turns and stops the words.

RISA
The voice that spoke those words belongs to Maxxus. It has been styled so by him that you will respond only to his real voice. It is not a trick. Your life has been controlled by his words. Here, listen to them again.

Risa turns the words on again.

MAXXUS (OC)
(recorded words)

You must obey only me. I am your savior. You trust only me. You will believe only me. Only I can make the world right again. You will worship me. You must vote for me in any election. I will save you. Anyone who does not believe me is an enemy. I am your master.

RISA
You have all been brainwashed. In an insidious feat of electronic and subsonic engineering, these commands have been fed directly into your brains by neurotransmission, without you even knowing it. His commands became your thoughts. His thoughts became your thoughts. His world became your world. And now the curtain has been pulled back. Now you can see how your lives have been controlled.

Risa turns in her chair and sets a series of controls on the master board.

RISA
I have set this podcast in a replay mode so that it will be transmitted in a continuous loop so that you can direct any other people who have been brainwashed by Maxxus to view it at their convenience.

CHASING THE DEAD

Inside the former interrogation room where Maxxus once sat. Now the shooter of Maxxus - a thing man in his mid 20s - is being questioned by Sld and Dr. Friedman.

SID
So, how can you be so sure that your shot did not kill the victim?

SHOOTER
There was no shot.

SID
What?

SHOOTER
I had him in range and a clear view. Then my gun jams. That damn guy is so lucky.

SID
Not as lucky as you think. He's dead.

SHOOTER
What! Not by me!

SID
Someone shot him from behind with a .357 magnum at close range.

SHOOTER 1
Shit! I wanted to kill him.

DR. FRIEDMAN
Why were you so determined to kill Maxxus?

SHOOTER (to Ted)

Like I told this other guy here before - so he could rise from the dead in 2 days.

Sudden revelation blanches Sid's face. He leaps toward the door.

SID
(pointing toward shooter)
Release him.

SHOOTER
And my rifle?

SID (over his shoulder)
No reason to hold it for evidence.

Sid races through the building, down a flight of stairs and bursts into the morgue. The body of Maxxus is stretched out on a long post mortem table. Ted joins Sid beside the table moments later.

DR. FRIEDMAN
What's this all about, Lieutenant?

SID
(trancelike)
I saw the wound having entered from the front. The coroner from the back. I assumed it was a rifle that was used. The corner said a handgun.

DR. FRIEDMAN
So?

SID
I saw the shooter being on the beach in the distance. The coroner assumed he was shot from close range on the pier.

DR. FRIEDMAN
I still don't see what you're driving at.

SID
And the shooter with the rifle couldn't have caused the wound because his gun jammed. And no one could have escaped the police patrol that was placed on the pier near the scene.

DR. FRIEDMAN
Which means?

SID
Maxxus was controlling our view of the situation and still does. What do you see before you now, Dr. Friedman?

DR. FRIEDMAN
A dead man on the table.

SID
Like the corpse of a fake hanging? Maxxus wants you to think he's dead. What I see is a swami. A master of illusion. A great, still living, magician.

Sid removes a pair of handcuffs and starts putting them on Maxxus' wrists but can only apply one cuff.

SID (to Maxxus)
I'm arresting you for the murder of your common law wife, Debbie Borges.

DR. FRIEDMAN
(shocked)
You're...you're arresting a corpse?

The eyes of Maxxus spring open.

MAXXUS (to Ted)
(smirking)
I'd hate to have you as a physician, Friedman. You can't even tell the living from the dead. And you, Lieutenant, should know you can't arrest a person who has been officially pronounced dead.

Maxxus leaps up from the table and, using the free unlocked portion of the heavy handcuff as a type of nunchuk (Asian weapon), begins swinging it and strikes both Sid and Ted in the heads, dazing both of them. Maxxus then flees the morgue and races out the front door, zigzagging down the long, straight sidewalk. Sid and Ted go in pursuit but are far behind.

SID
He sure can run for a corpse, Doc.

Rifle shot rings out. Maxxus falls to the ground.

DR. FRIEDMAN
I don't think I've ever seen anybody who's been shot at so many times.

An ordinary looking car pulls up to a nearby curb, the front passenger side door opens and the shooter who'd just been released hops in. Captain Simmons is at the driver's wheel.

CAPTAIN SIMMONS (to shooter)
Dead? You sure?

SHOOTER
Yes, sir. He's as dead as they come.

CAPTAIN SIMMONS
A commendation is waiting.

SHOOTER
They don't hand those out in our division, you know that. A mission well done is its own reward.

Captain Simmons and the shooter speed away in their escape vehicle..

MANY DAYS

Next day, assembled in Myers' office; the lieutenant. behind his desk and Ted, Risa and Carlos seated around the room. Risa and Carlos have their chairs touching side by side in a very familiar manner.

DR. FRIEDMAN (to Sid)
And the real killer of Maxxus got away?

SID
Yes. No witnesses. Nothing.

CARLOS (to Sid)
Do you think it was the same shooter you talked to in the warehouse?

SID
Can't say.

DR. FRIEDMAN
Or won't?

SID
Either way. A person can't be convicted of shooting a corpse. What's the point of apprehending him?

Carlos and Risa exclaim "What!" in unison.

DR. FRIEDMAN
Maxxus was pronounced DOA by the coroner after being shot at the pier. The Lt. moved to arrest him from the slab in the morgue anyway and Maxxus got up and ran off.

RISA

If he was dead...how?

DR. FRIEDMAN
I'll explain it all to you later in the official briefing. In simple terms, he made most of us all believe he was really dead. The Lieutenant figured it out.

SID
Yes, I recalled the story of the man who could make people believe he was dead by hanging himself, but made a mistake one time and did too good of a job of it - hung himself for real. Maxxus faked his own death well.

DR. FRIEDMAN (to Risa)
And you Sergeant Sanchez: how did you arrange for that miracle podcast that revealed the command words that Maxxus used to brainwash his followers?

RISA
Maxxus left a couple of original source copies of his voice that he would later transfer into infrasound code. He used the copies to make additions to or to tweak his control phrases. I found their location on his server and played the words at normal speed and sound level for his cult members.

SID
Infrasound?

RISA
A pitch at such extremely low wavelength that it is beyond human hearing.

DR. FRIEDMAN
Exceptional work, Sergeant.

RISA
I also found audio proof that Maxxus caused the death of Ms. Borges. He'd coded a specialized message he sent to all the women he wanted to be rid of. The words - Cast You Out - Forever - translate into you must kill yourself. Do it now.

SID
Excellent. So we got him dead to rights on all counts.

CARLOS
One thing about all of this still haunts me: the last words that Maxxus said on the beach when he convinced us all he was dying.

DR. FRIEDMAN
Oh? What were they?

CARLOS
He said something about taking solace in the belief that he would still be alive in another universe. And he didn't mean heaven.

DR. FRIEDMAN
I see. He could've been referring to the multiverse or Many Worlds theory as developed by the brilliant quantum physicist Hugh Everett III

CARLOS
What exactly is that?

DR. FRIEDMAN
Basically it states that during one's life a person comes to various crossroads or decisive points where that one choice they make at that time can have multiple effects. The choice made then creates a new pathway to develop which that person follows, as his true other self, in that other universe.

CARLOS
So this means that all of us are living, as ourselves, right now in a different universe or universes?

DR. FRIEDMAN
Correct.

CARLOS
That's a pretty wild theory.

DR. FRIEDMAN
Many people believe it.

SID
Well, right now I've got enough problems in this universe to worry about rather than what I'll be doing in all of the

others. Writing up a report on this whole situation is one of them. But that's for later.

RISA
Hopefully Detective Montoya and myself can add a little light and maybe hope to this dark story.

CARLOS
Should we tell them?

RISA
We're going to look into the possibility of adopting Ms. Borges's little girl. I'd like to be her new soccer mom, if she'd let me.

SID
(great surprise)
The 2 of you! Since when?

DR. FRIEDMAN (to Myers)
You don't keep up on Department news, do you Lieutenant? Didn't you know that these 2 spent a couple years together in data collection and processing?

SID
Even the best of us have something to learn - right, Detective Montoya?

CARLOS
Right, sir. I guess in one way or another we're all rookies.

SID

Speaking of which, the Dodgers have a new rookie pitcher and I plan to be at that game tonight. I want to put this case behind me.

Sid gets up and starts toward the door.

DR. FRIEDMAN

I don't blame you. What about this pitcher?

SID

Yeah, they say he's got a blazing fastball.

DR. FRIEDMAN

Blazing? As in fiery? Could explode at any minute?

Carlos and Risa stifle chuckles.

SID

(clears throat)

Yeah, well, I've heard his curve ball is so deceptive that it seems to disappear before reaching home plate.

DR. FRIEDMAN

Like a sleight of hand trick by a great magician?

Led by Myers the group heads toward the door.

SID

(grunts)

Yes, uh, but he's supposed to have a changeup that makes a batter so off balance that some of them duck out of the batter's box.

DR. FRIEDMAN
Like the misdirection of a magic...(cannot hear the end
of the sentence as they all exit the office.)

All exit the office and the door closes behind them.

THE   END